OPERATIC ARIAS

Midi Piano Library

Exclusive Distributors:

Music Sales Limited
8/9 Frith Street,
London W1V 5TZ, England.

Music Sales Corporation
257 Park Avenue South
New York, NY10010
United States of America.

Music Sales Pty Limited
120 Rothschild Avenue,
Rosebery, NSW 2018,
Australia.

Order No.AM91786
ISBN 0-7119-3911-X
This book © Copyright 1994 by Wise Publications

Unauthorised reproduction of any part of this publication by any means including photocopying is an infringement of copyright.

Book & pack design by 4i Limited
Arrangements by Paul Lawley
Music processed by Interactive Sciences Limited

Printed in the United Kingdom by
Caligraving Limited, Thetford, Norfolk.

Photographs courtesy of:
London Features International

Your Guarantee of Quality

As publishers, we strive to produce every book to the highest commercial standards. The music has been freshly engraved and this book has been carefully designed to minimise awkward page turns and to make playing from it a real pleasure. Throughout, the printing and binding have been planned to ensure a sturdy, attractive publication which should give years of enjoyment. If your copy fails to meet our high standards, please inform us and we will gladly replace it.

Music Sales' complete catalogue describes thousands of titles and is available in full colour sections by subject, direct from Music Sales Limited. Please state your areas of interest and send a cheque/postal order for £1.50 for postage to: Music Sales Limited, Newmarket Road, Bury St. Edmunds, Suffolk IP33 3YB.

PREFACE	5
FAIREST ISLE, ALL ISLES EXCELLING	6
HABANERA	18
HERE AM I IN HER BOUDOIR	8
LA DONNA È MOBILE	10
ON WITH THE MOTLEY	12
POUR, O LOVE, SWEET CONSOLATION	14
THE BIRDCATCHER'S SONG	16
THE FLOWER SONG	21
TOREADOR'S SONG	24
TREASURED MEM'RY OF HIS NAME	26
WHEN I AM LAID IN EARTH	28
WHEN I HAVE OFTEN HEARD	30

PREFACE

Included with this book you will find a brand new kind of music data disk. On this 3.5" disk are digitally recorded Standard Midi Files (SMF). These files or songs can be played on any dedicated or Computer based Standard Midi File player which conforms to the General MIDI system (GM).

The files contain professionally recorded piano accompaniments plus full backing orchestration. You can either listen to, or play along with the accompaniment. The right-hand of the piano is on Midi Channel 4 and the left-hand on Midi Channel 3. According to the instructions for your particular player you can mute the relevant channel and then practise each hand separately.

PREFACE

Ce livre est accompagné d'une disquette de données musicales d'un style tout nouveau. En effet, cette disquette de 3,5" contient des fichiers MIDI standards (Standard MIDI Files, ou SMF) enregistrés par procédé numérique. Ces fichiers, ou morceaux, peuvent être lus par n'importe quel lecteur SFM dédié ou informatisé se conformant aux normes MIDI.

Les fichiers comprennent une mélodie au piano et un accompagnement orchestral de haute qualité pour chacun des morceaux. Vous pouvez simplement écouter ces derniers, ou bien jouer en même temps. Le piano est réparti entre les deux canaux MIDI – la main droite sur le canal 4 et la main gauche sur le canal 3. Vous pouvez donc couper l'un des deux canaux (en suivant les instructions pour votre machine) afin d'exercer chaque main séparément.

VORWORT

Diesem Notenbuch ist eine völlig neue Art von Musikdaten-Diskette beigelegt. Die 3,5" Diskette enthält digital aufgezeichnete Standard MIDI Files (SMF), die dem General MIDI (GM)-System entsprechen. Diese Files oder Musiktitel können auf jedem Sequenzer, der in der Lage ist, SMF-Daten zu lesen, abgespielt werden.

Die einzelnen Musiktitel enthalten zum Klavier-Part eine professionell arrangierte Begleitung. Sie können sich diese Musik anhören oder selbst zu den Arrangements spielen. Die Noten für die rechte Hand des Klavier-Parts sind auf MIDI Kanal 4, die für den Part der linken Hand auf MIDI-Kanal 3 aufgezeichnet.

Bitte beachten Sie die Bedienhinweise zu Ihrem Sequenzer, um den MIDI-Kanal oder die entsprechende Spur stumm zu schalten, damit Sie die rechte und linke Hand separat zur Begleitung spielen können.

PREFACIO

Incluido en este libro vd. encontrará un tipo completamente nuevo de disco de datos musicales. En este disco de 3.5" hay Standard Midi Files (SMF) grabados digitalmente. Estos ficheros o canciones pueden ser reproducidos en cualquier reproductor de Standard Midi Files diseñado para allo o basado en ordenador que se ajuste al sistema General MIDI (GM).

Los ficheros contienen acompañamientos de piano grabados profesionalmente además de una completa orquestación. Vd. puede o bien escuchar o bien tocar junto con el acompañamiento. La mano derecha del piano está en Canal Midi 4 y la mano izquierda en Canal Midi 3. De acuerdo con las instrucciones de su reproductor particular Vd. puede enmudecer el canal oportuno y practicar cada mano separadamente.

PREMESSA

Incluso in questo libro. troverete un nuovo tipo di dati musicali su disco. In questo dischetto da 3,5" sono memorizzati Standard Midi File (SMF). Questi file o canzoni possono essere riprodotti su qualsiasi lettore dedicato o computerizzato in grado di riconoscere gli Standard Midi File conformi allle specifiche del sistema General Midi (GM).

I file contengono registrazioni professionali di accompagnamento di pianoforte complete di orchestrazione strumentale. E' possibile suonare insieme alla parte di accompagnamento o anche semplicemente ascoltare il brano. La parte della mano destra per pianoforte è memorizzata sul Canale Midi 4, quella della mano sinistra sul Canale Midi 3. A seconda dell'esigenza del singolo esecutore e possibile ammutolire (mute) il rispettivo canale delle due parti e esercitare separatamente mano destra e mano sinistra.

Fairest Isle, All Isles Excelling
from King Arthur
Composed by Henry Purcell (1659–1695)

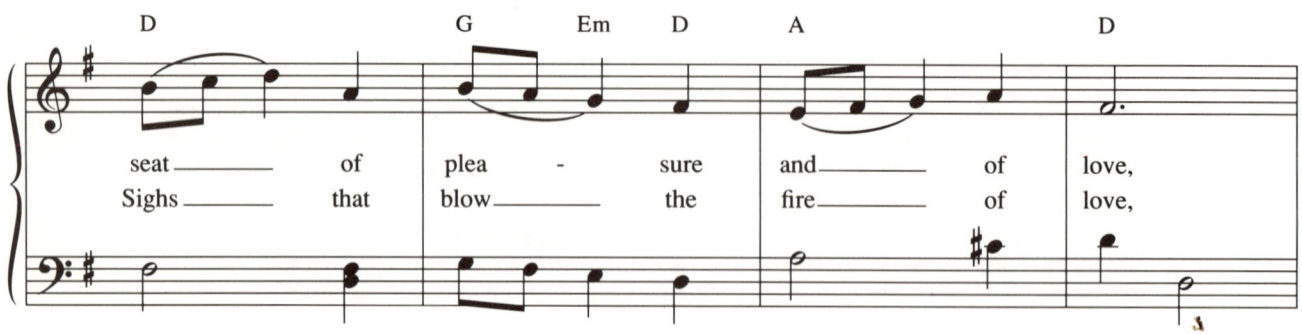
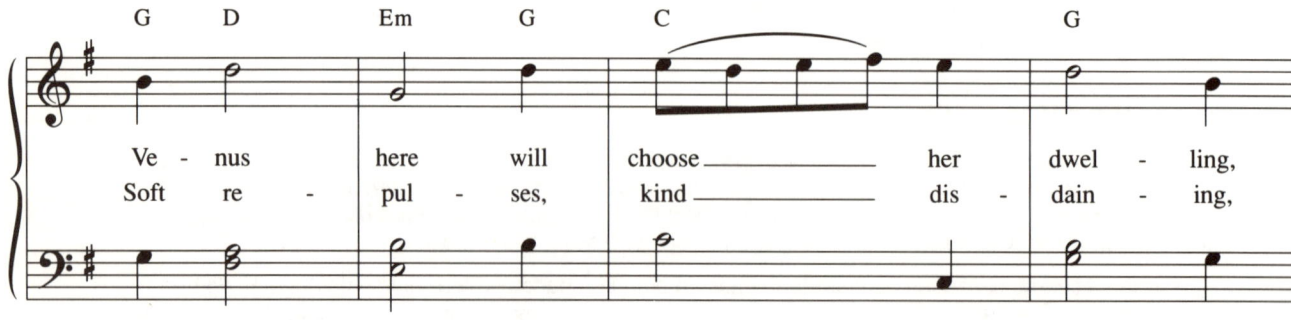

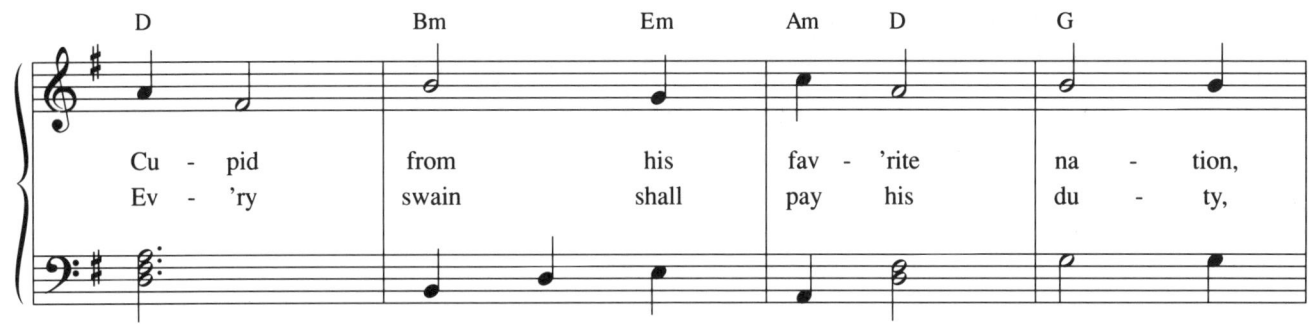
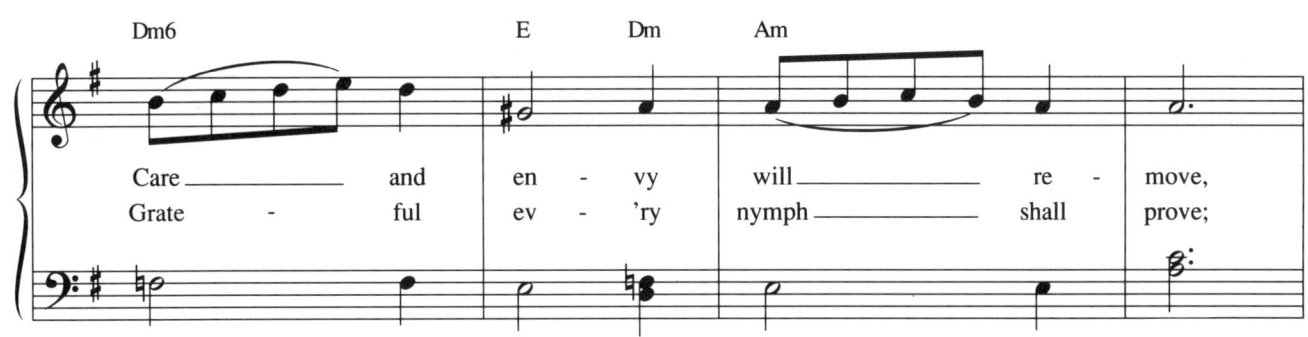
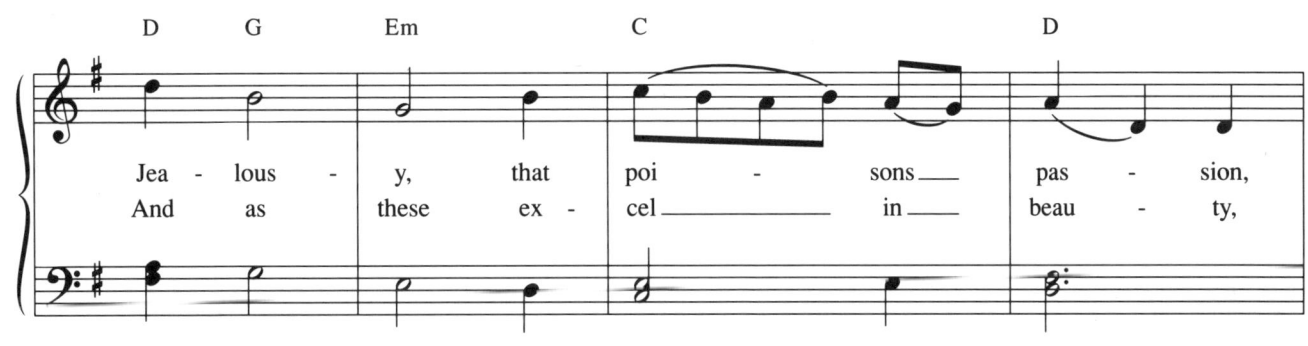
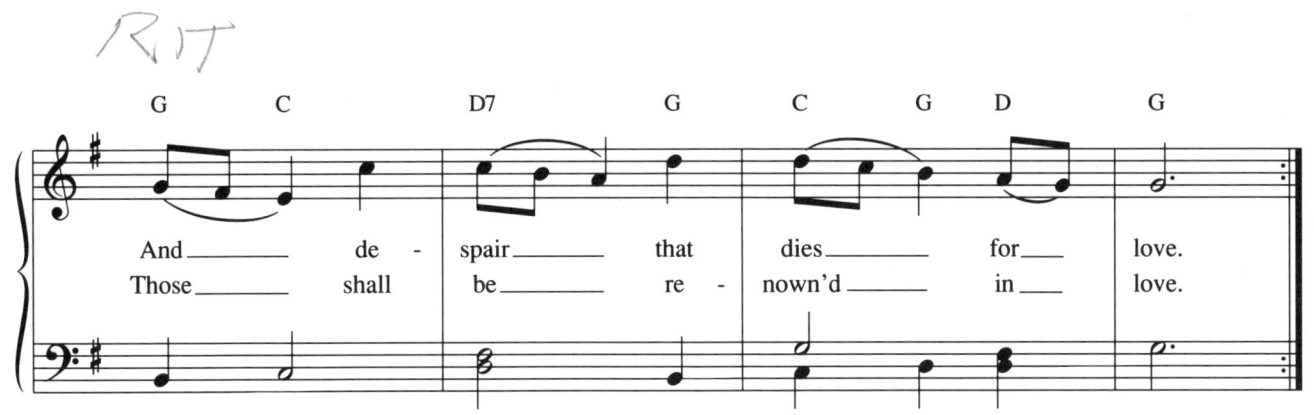

Here Am I In Her Boudoir
from Mignon
Composed by Ambroise Thomas (1811–1896)

La Donna è Mobile
from Rigoletto
Composed by Giuseppe Verdi (1813–1901)

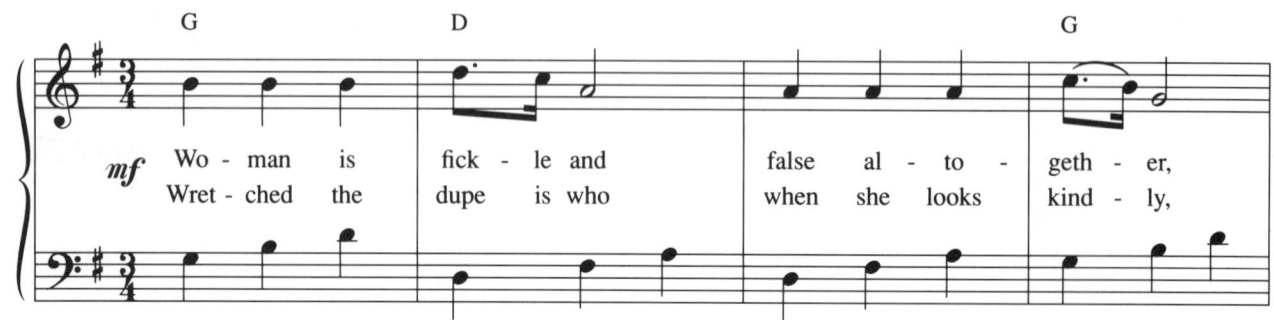

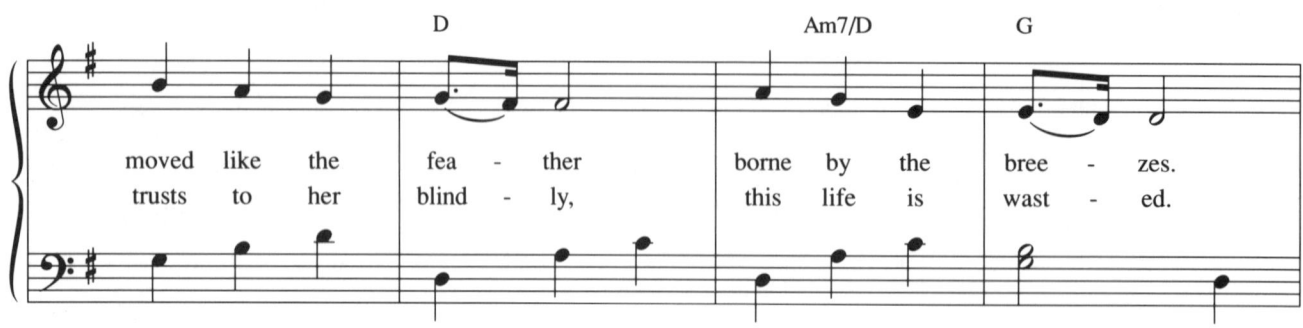

On With The Motley

from I Pagliacci

Composed by Ruggiero Leoncavallo (1858–1919)

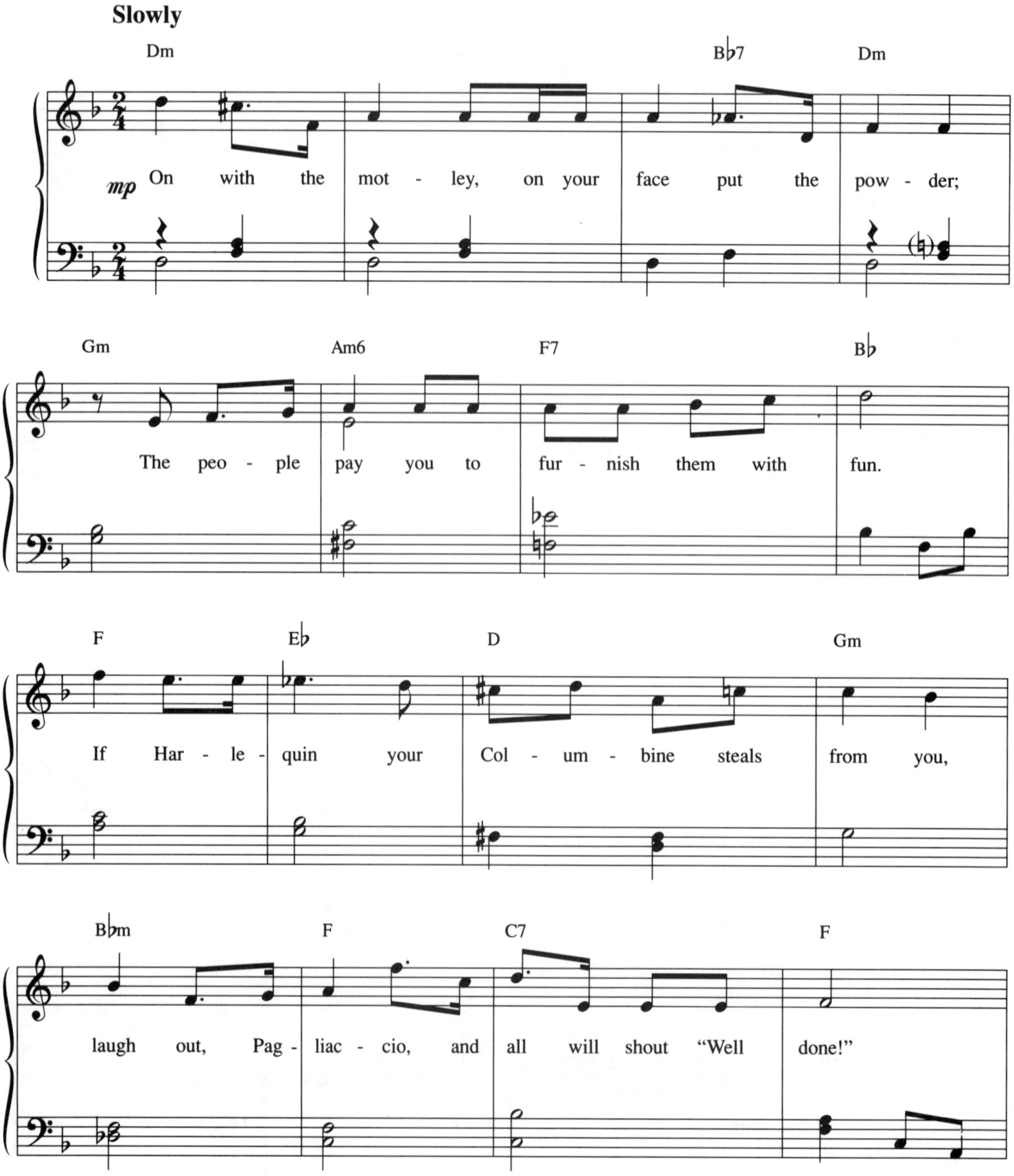

Pour, O Love, Sweet Consolation
from The Marriage Of Figaro
Composed by Wolfgang Amadeus Mozart (1756–1791)

The Birdcatcher's Song
from The Magic Flute
Composed by Wolfgang Amadeus Mozart (1756–1791)

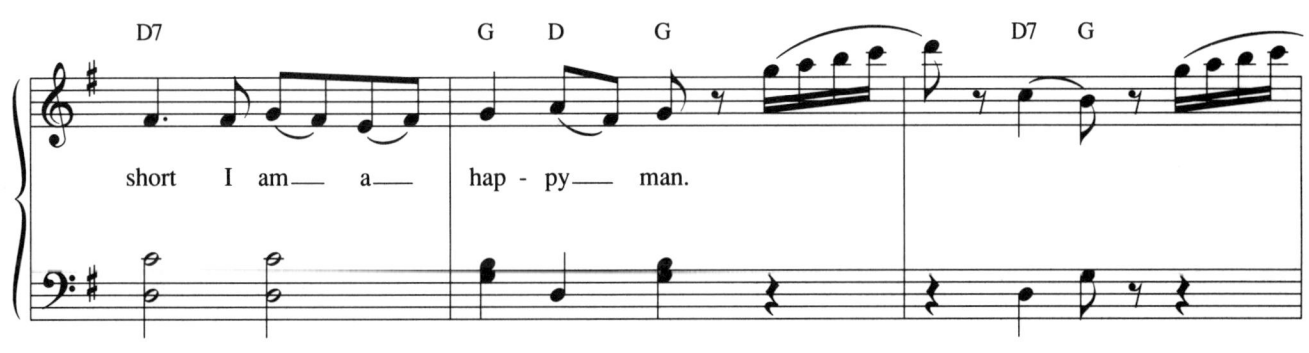
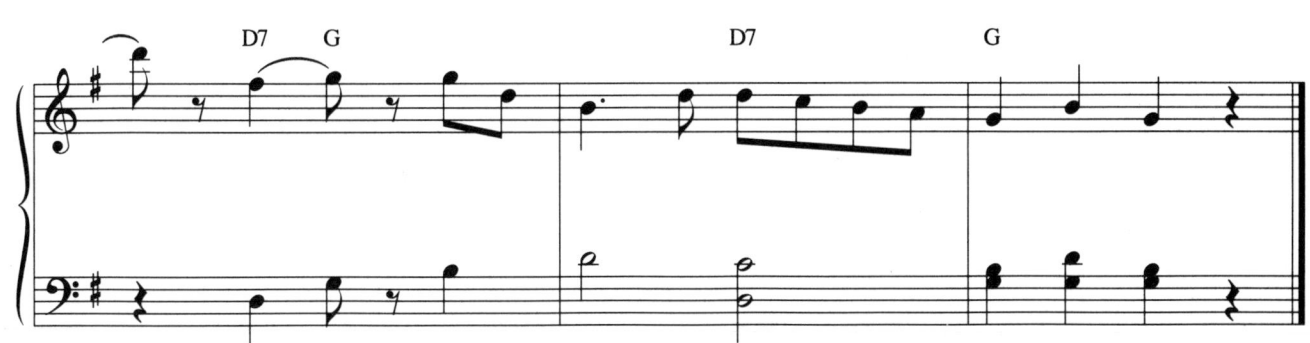

Habanera
from Carmen
Composed by Georges Bizet (1838–1875)

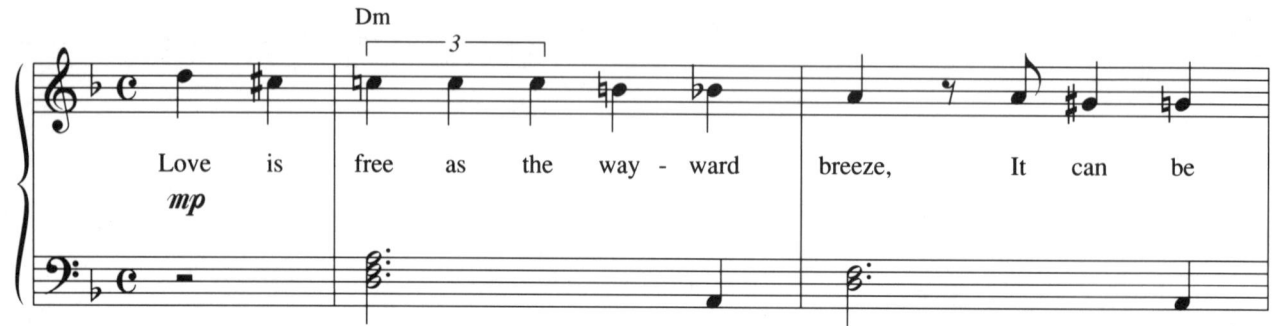
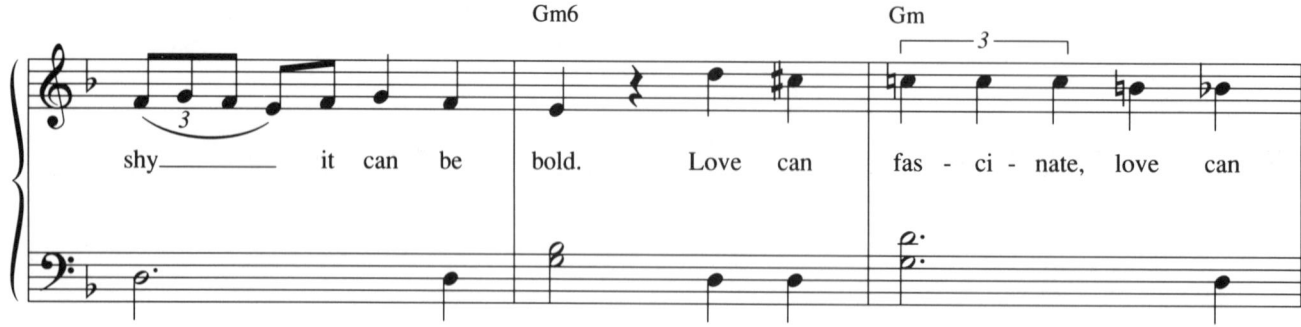
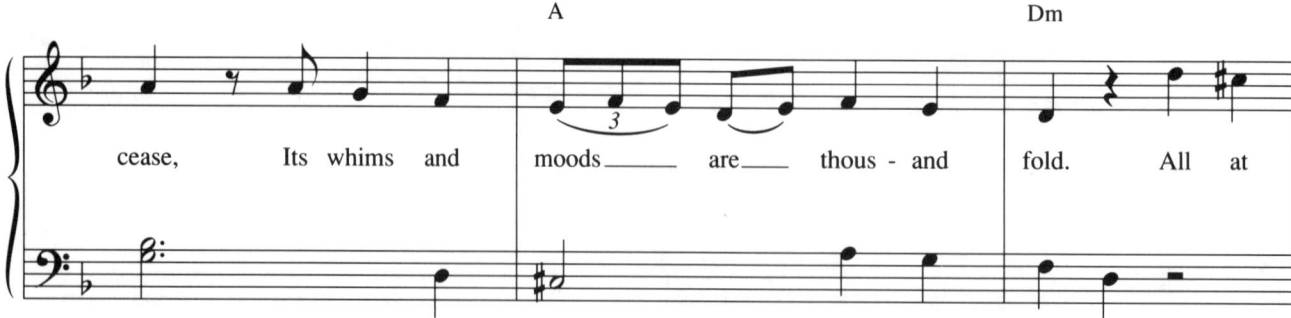
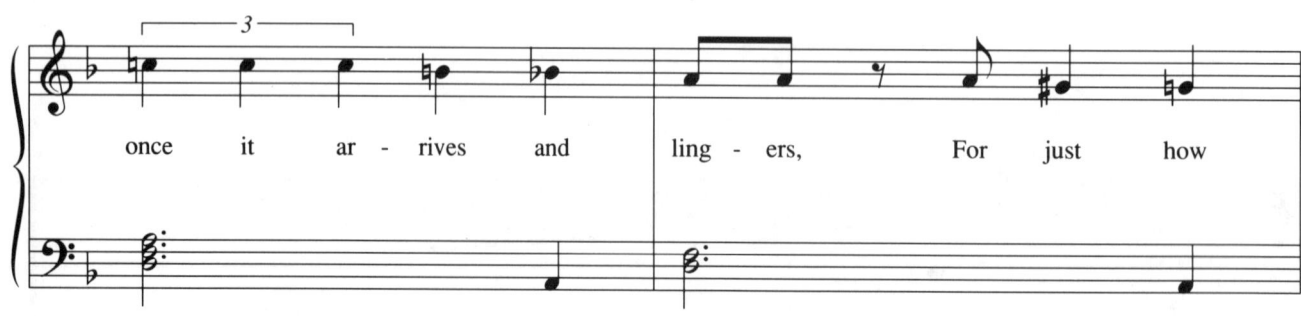

The Flower Song
from Carmen
Composed by Georges Bizet (1838–1875)

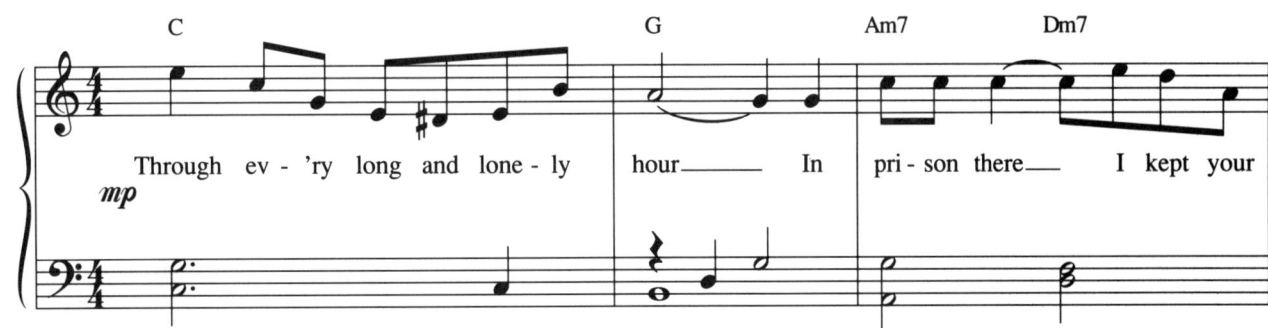

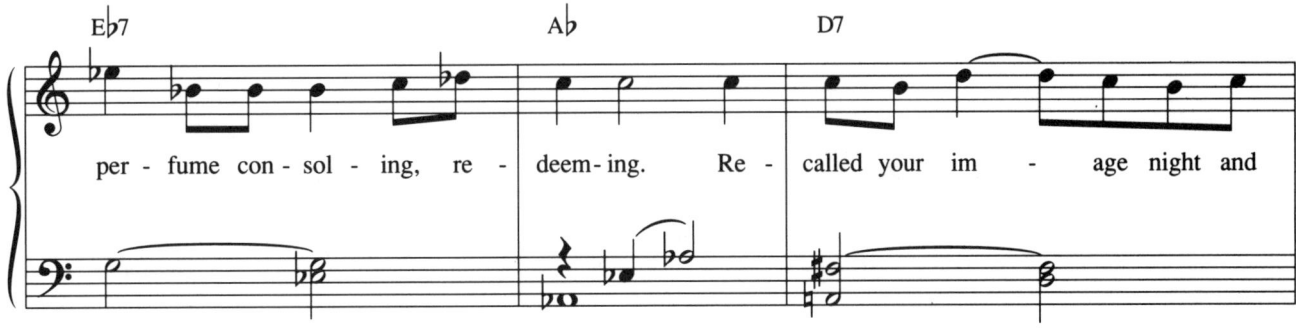

© Copyright 1994 Dorsey Brothers Music Limited, 8/9 Frith Street, London W1.
All Rights Reserved. International Copyright Secured.

Toreador's Song
from Carmen
Composed by Georges Bizet (1838–1875)

Treasured Mem'ry Of His Name
from Rigoletto
Composed by Giuseppe Verdi (1813–1901)

When I Am Laid In Earth
from Dido And Aeneas
Composed by Henry Purcell (1659–1695)

When I Have Often Heard
from The Faery Queen
Composed by Henry Purcell (1659–1695)

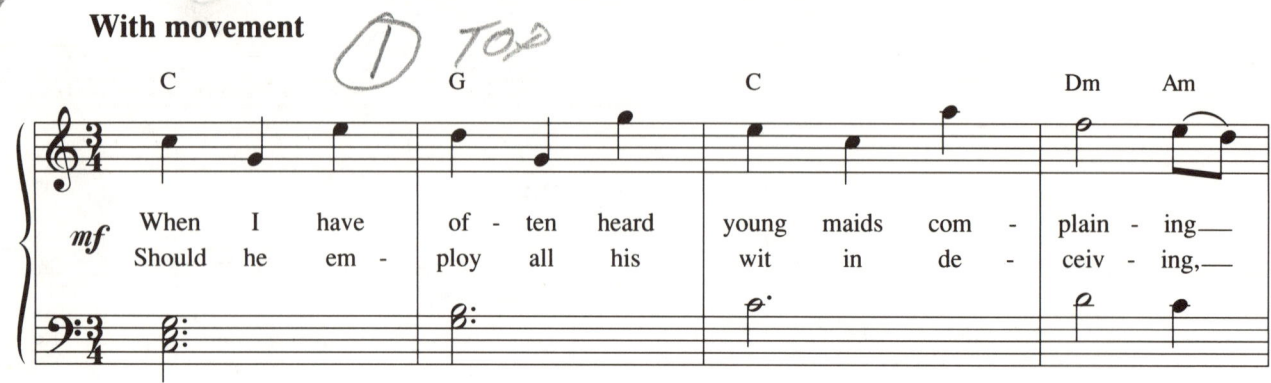
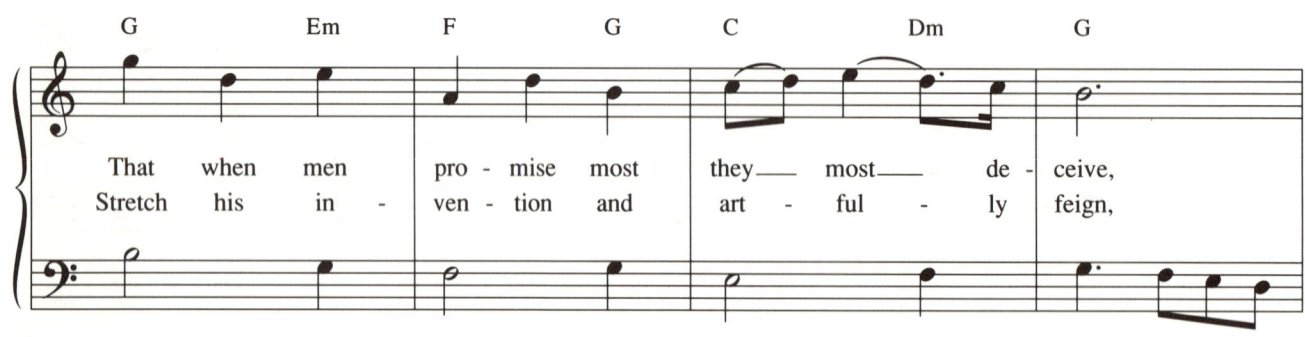
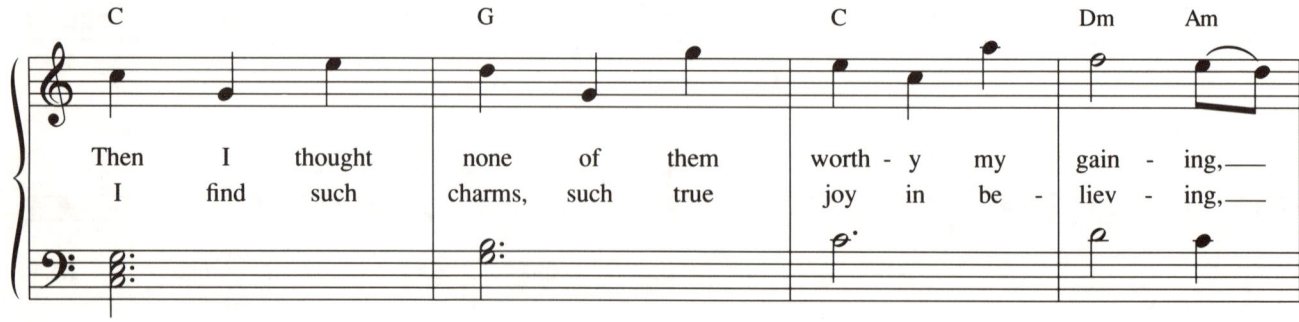
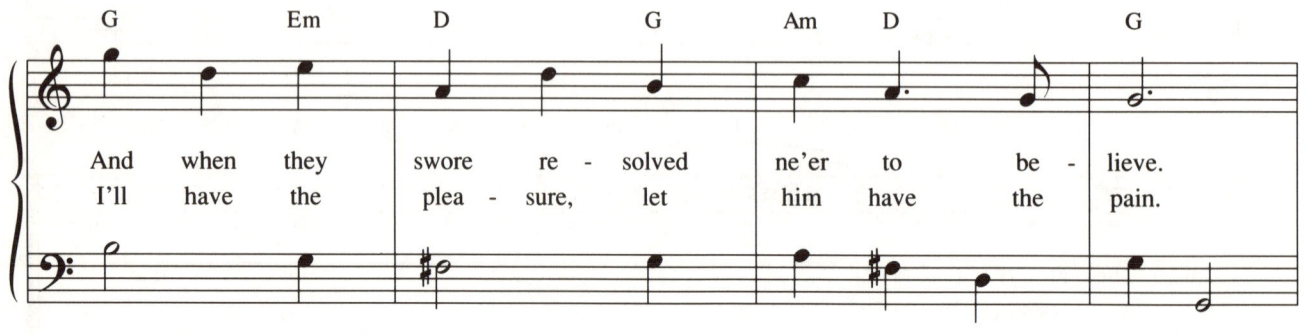

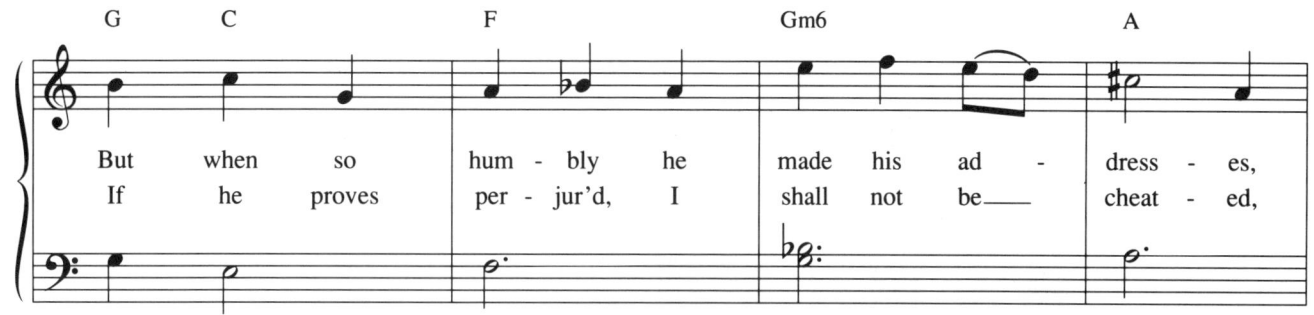
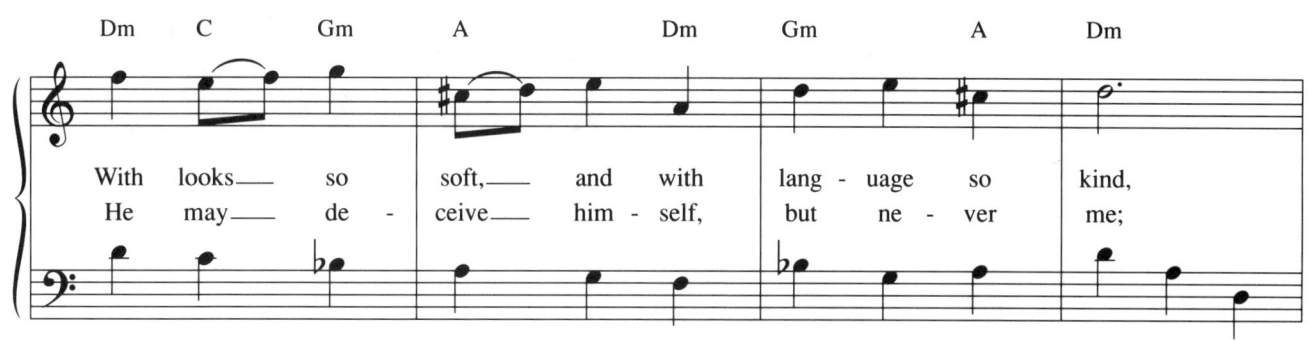
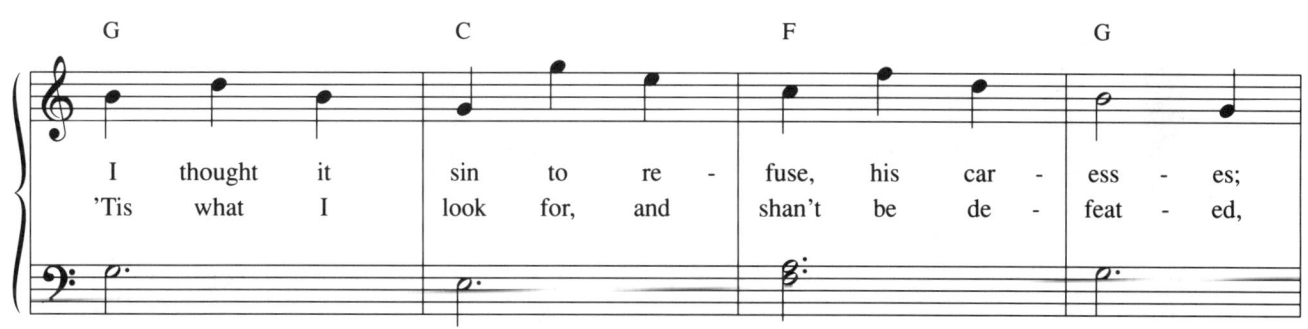
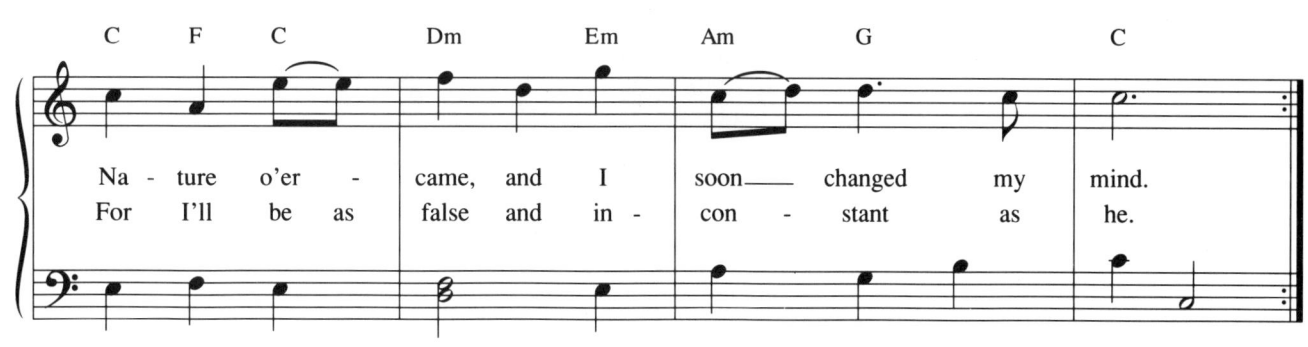

The Beatles

Enya

Phil Collins

Van Morrison

Bob Dylan

Sting

Paul Simon

Tracy Chapman

Eric Clapton

Pink Floyd

New Kids On The Block

Bryan Adams   Tina Turner   Elton John

Bee Gees   Whitney Houston   AC/DC

Bringing you the words

All the latest in rock and pop. Plus the brightest and best in West End show scores. Music books for every instrument under the sun. And exciting new teach-yourself ideas like "Let's Play Keyboard" - in cassette/book packs, or on video. Available from all good music shops.

and music

Music Sales' complete catalogue lists thousands of titles and is available free from your local music shop, or direct from Music Sales Limited. Please send a cheque or postal order for £1.50 (for postage) to:

Music Sales Limited
Newmarket Road,
Bury St Edmunds,
Suffolk IP33 3YB

Buddy

Five Guys Named Moe

Les Misérables

West Side Story

Phantom Of The Opera

Show Boat

The Rocky Horror Show

Bringing you the world's best music.